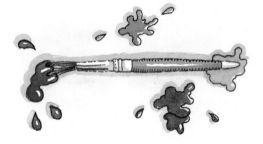

First published 1993 by
Walker Books Ltd
87 Vauxhall Walk
London SE11 5HJ

This edition published 1996

2 4 6 8 10 9 7 5 3 1

Text © 1993 Vivian French
Illustrations © 1993 Chris Fisher

Printed in England

ISBN 0-7445-3378-3

PAINTER BEAR

Written by Vivian French

Illustrated by Chris Fisher

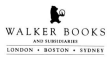

WALKER BOOKS
AND SUBSIDIARIES

LONDON · BOSTON · SYDNEY

Oh, Painter Bear, what a mess!
Time to wash and change
your clothes.

Time to put on a blue T-shirt

and red trousers.

A yellow sock
and a green one.

Orange slippers

and a big purple hat.

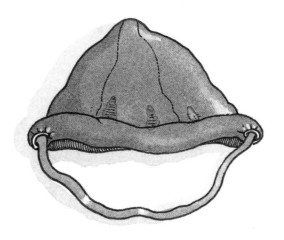

What are you looking for now,
Painter Bear? A paintbrush?

Oh, Painter Bear, what a mess!

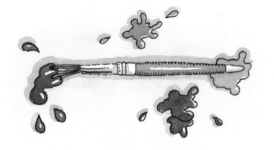